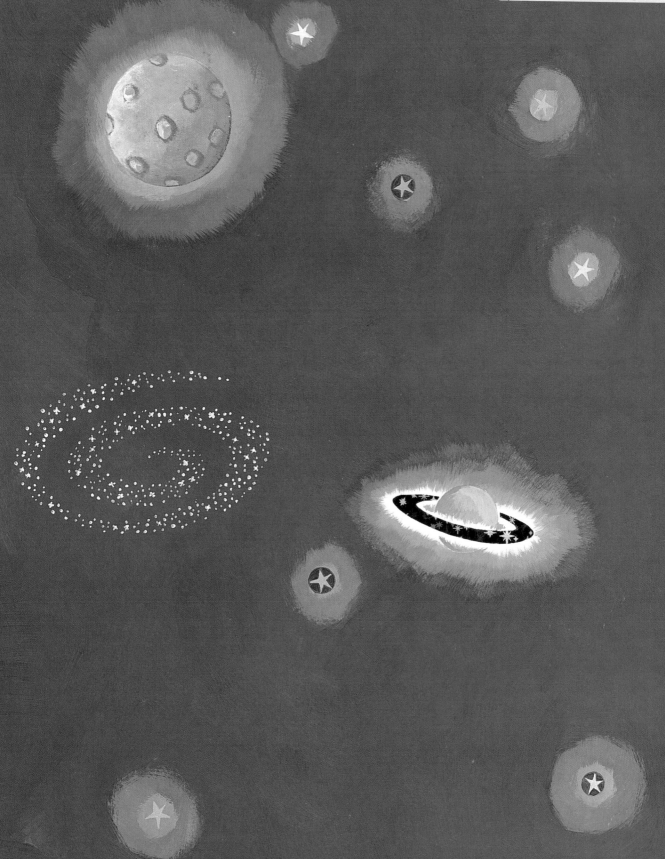

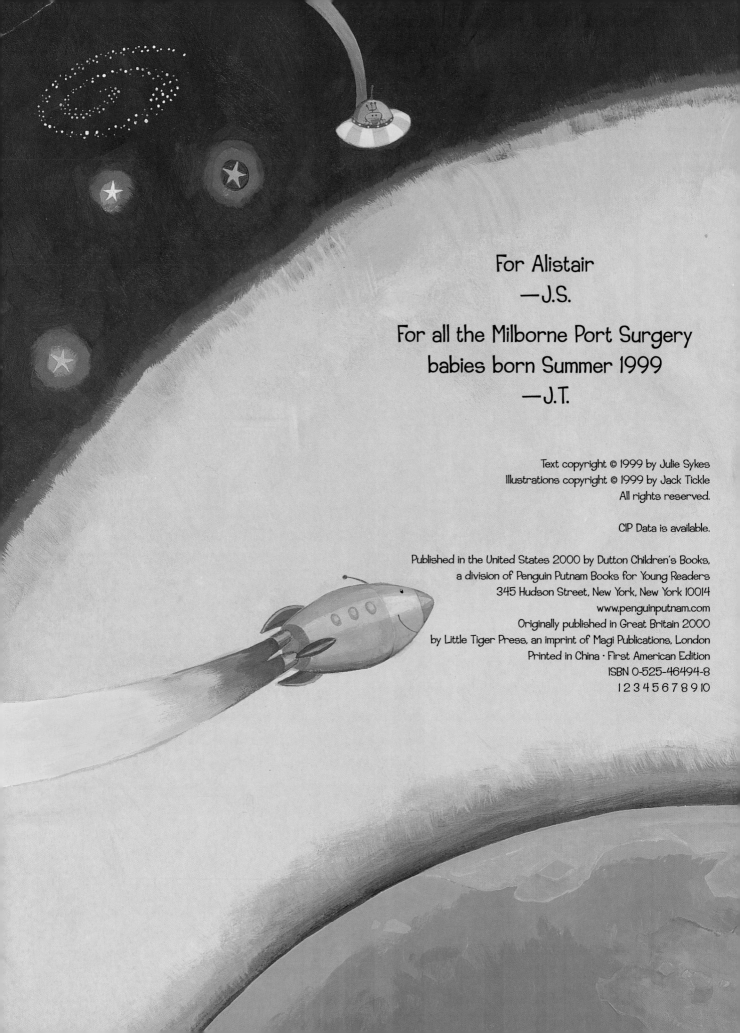

For Alistair
—J.S.

For all the Milborne Port Surgery
babies born Summer 1999
—J.T.

Text copyright © 1999 by Julie Sykes
Illustrations copyright © 1999 by Jack Tickle
All rights reserved.

CIP Data is available.

Published in the United States 2000 by Dutton Children's Books,
a division of Penguin Putnam Books for Young Readers
345 Hudson Street, New York, New York 10014
www.penguinputnam.com
Originally published in Great Britain 2000
by Little Tiger Press, an imprint of Magi Publications, London
Printed in China · First American Edition
ISBN 0-525-46494-8
1 2 3 4 5 6 7 8 9 10

Little ROCKET'S Special Star

by **JULIE SYKES**

illustrated by **JACK TICKLE**

Dutton Children's Books
New York

Little Rocket and her dad, Big Joe, loved looking up at the stars.
    Tomorrow was Big Joe's birthday, and Little Rocket wanted to give him something very special. *I know,* she thought. *I'll give him a shiny star all his own.*

Very early the next morning, while Big
Joe was resting on his launchpad, Little
Rocket set off—WHOOSH—into space. Up,
up, up she flew until she could see
something small and glittering high above.

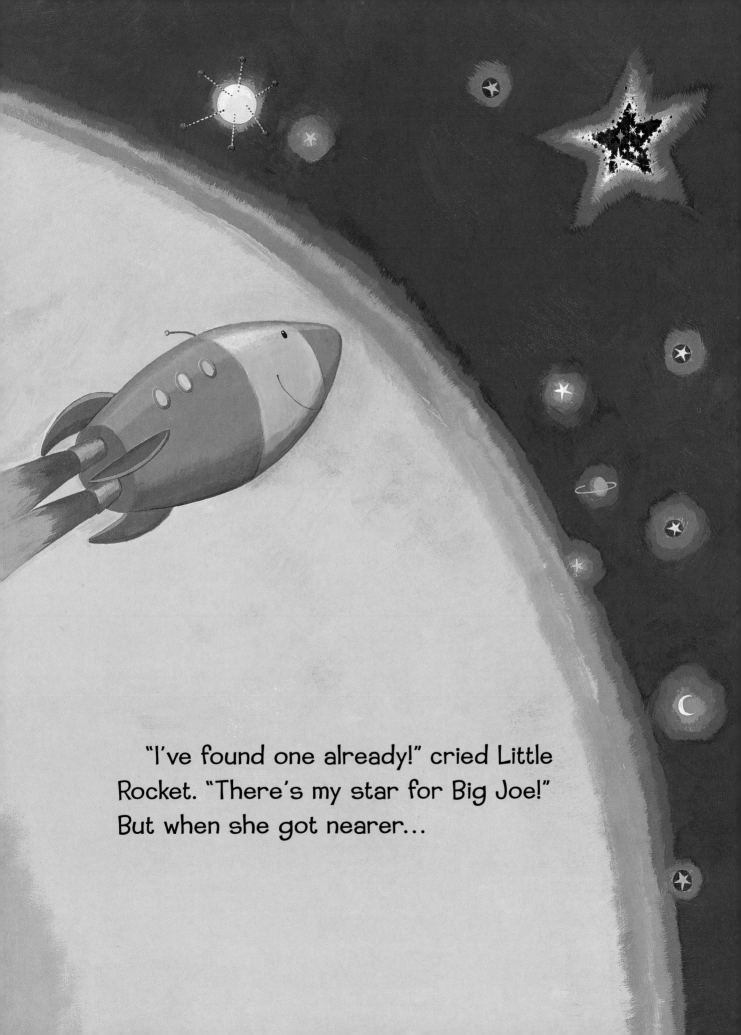

"I've found one already!" cried Little Rocket. "There's my star for Big Joe!" But when she got nearer...

she found it wasn't a star at all!
It was Satellite Sid, circling the
Earth. "What are you doing out
here, Little Rocket?" he asked.
"I'm looking for a star for Big
Joe," said Little Rocket.

"You can't take a star from the sky," said
Satellite Sid. "It would be too hot to carry."

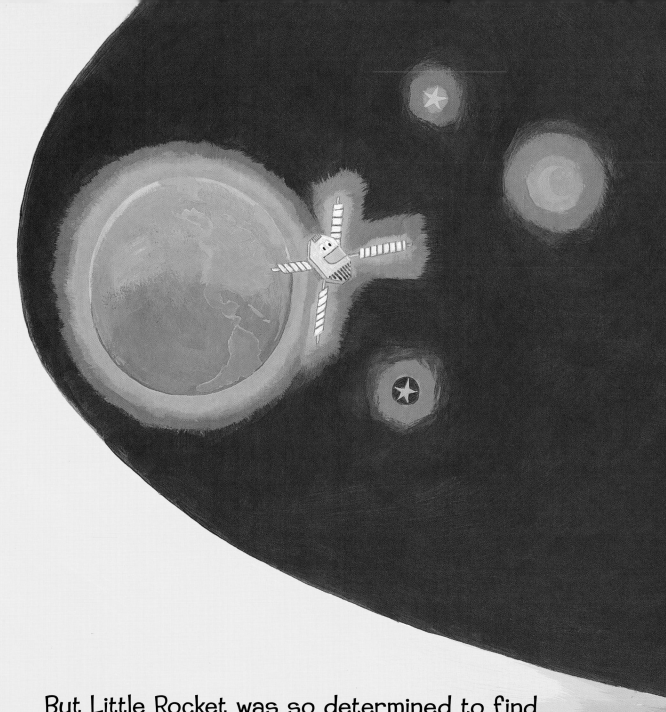

But Little Rocket was so determined to find
a star for Big Joe that she didn't believe him.
"You're wrong," she said, and WHIZZ—off she
flew again, higher and higher and higher.

Suddenly Little Rocket saw something
winking in the darkness. "A star!" she cried,
flying quickly toward it. But when she got
nearer...

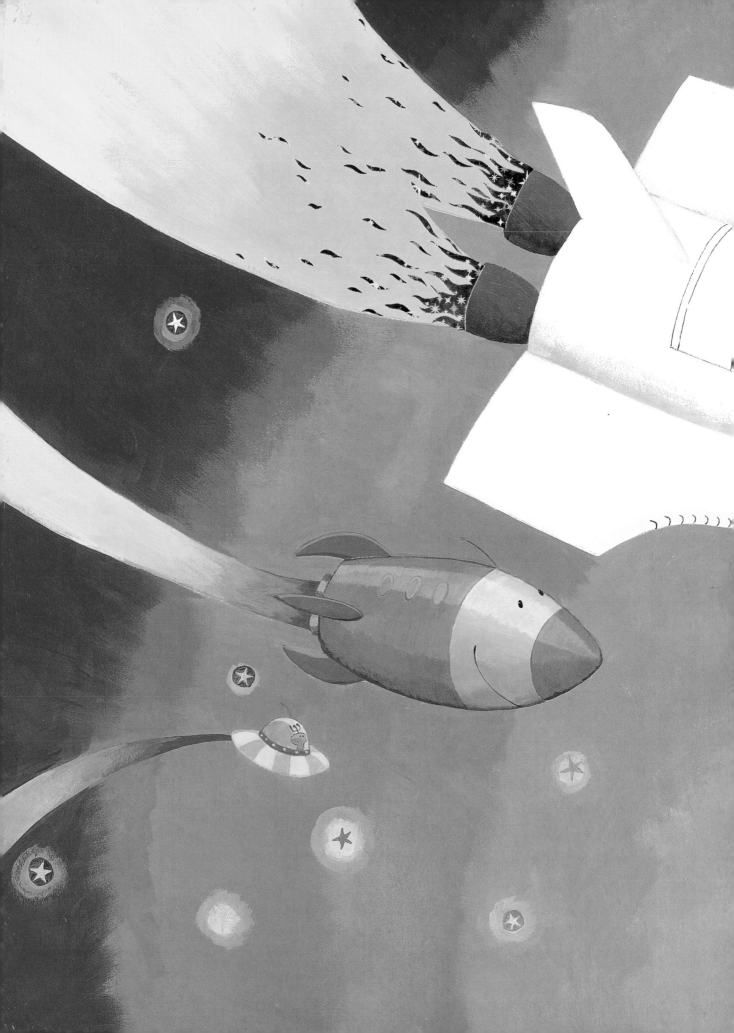

she saw it was only the flames
from Sammy Shuttle's engines.

"Hello, Little Rocket," said Sammy.
"What a surprise!"

"I thought you were a star," said
Little Rocket. "I want one for Big
Joe."

"You can't take a star," said
Sammy. "They might look small from
far away, but stars are very big.
You wouldn't be able to carry it."

Little Rocket thought Sammy must be mistaken. "Yes, I would!" she said confidently. "Besides, I only want one little star."

Off she ZOOMED again, on her way. She hadn't gone far before she spotted a tiny, flickering light. "A little star!" she cried, but as she flew closer to it, she found...

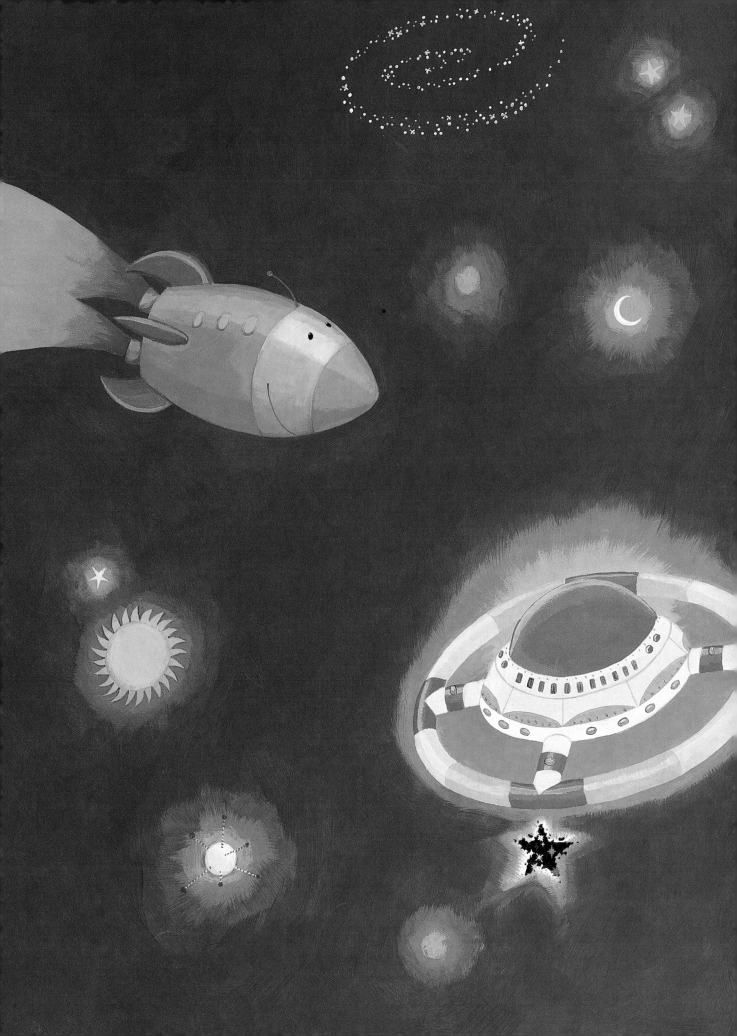

it was only Andy the Astronaut's flashlight. He was shining it on the space station as he made repairs.

"You nearly knocked me over," said Andy. "Where are you going in such a hurry?"

"I'm looking for a star for Big Joe's birthday."

"The stars are much too far away. It would take years to reach them," said Andy, laughing.

"I'll reach them!" boasted Little Rocket. "Flying to the moon doesn't take so long. The stars can't be much farther."

And with a WHOOSH, Little Rocket flew faster and faster toward the moon! On its surface, she could see something glimmering.

"Is it a star?" she wondered, feeling a little uncertain. As she got nearer…

she saw it wasn't a star. It was
another little spaceship, stuck in
a crater!

"Hang on," she called, landing
beside him. "I'll get you out."

Little Rocket tugged and pushed and shoved
and pulled until POP!

The little spaceship slid free!

"My wing is bent," he wailed. "I don't know if I
can fly." Little Rocket wanted to continue looking
for a star for Big Joe, but she knew she couldn't
leave this broken spaceship all alone.

"Don't worry. I'll tow you home," she said.

It was hard work pulling the
little spaceship, and Little Rocket
was worried about not having a
present for Big Joe.

But she did enjoy the amazed looks they got as they flew past Andy Astronaut...

and Sammy Shuttle...

and Satellite Sid.

At last they landed with a BUMP beside Big Joe.

"Where have you been?" he asked. "And what's happened to this poor little spaceship?"

Little Rocket told him about the special star, and about how she had rescued the broken spaceship instead.

"Good job, Little Rocket," said Big Joe. "It's better to help someone than to bring me a present. Besides, the stars belong in space, where everyone can enjoy them.

"I already have a star, you know," he added.

"You do?"

"Yes, I do," said Big Joe.

"Little Rocket, *you* are
my very special star!"

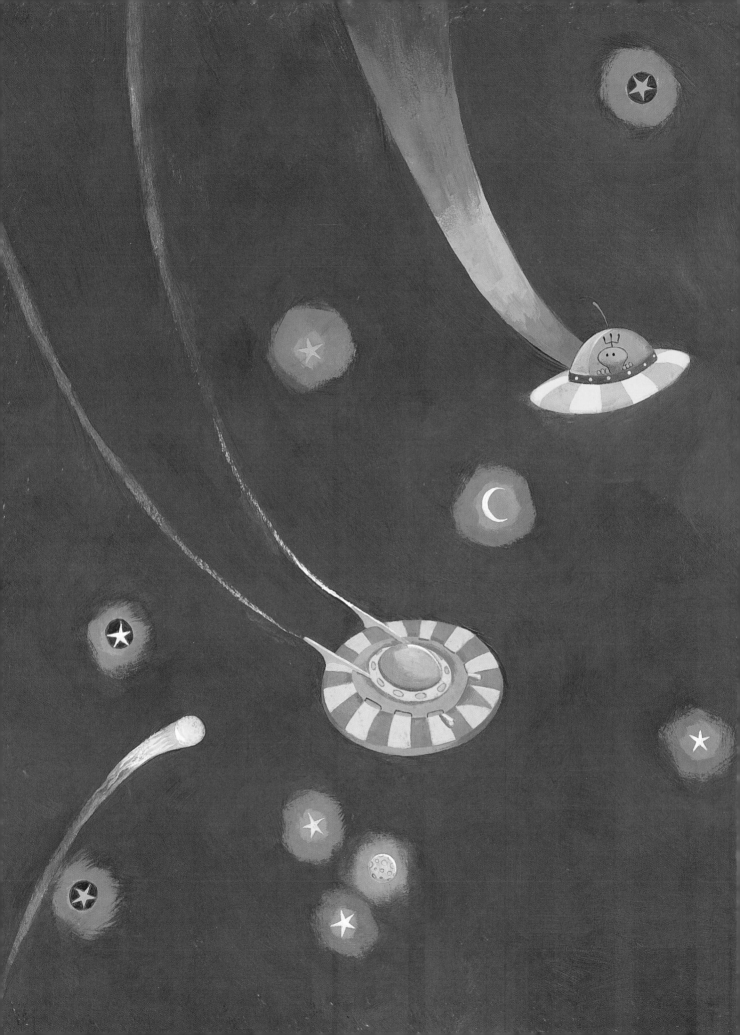